sound/hammer

also by Dennis Barone

poetry
Parallel Lines
Separate Objects
Forms / Froms

prose
On the Bus: Selected Stories
Field Report
North Arrow
Precise Machine
God's Whisper
The Walls of Circumstance
Temple of the Rat
Echoes
The Returns
Abusing the Telephone

criticism
America / Trattabili

editor
Garnet Poems: An Anthology of Connecticut Poetry Since 1776
Essays on Italian American Literature and Culture (with Peter Covino)
New Hungers for Old: One-Hundred Years of Italian-American Poetry
Small Towns, Big Cities: The Urban Experience of Italian Americans (with Stefano Luconi)
Visiting Wallace: Poems Inspired by the Life and Work of Wallace Stevens (with James Finnegan)
Furnished Rooms by Emanuel Carnevali
Beyond the Red Notebook: Essays on Paul Auster
The Art of Practice: Forty-Five Contemporary Poets (with Peter Ganick)

sound/hammer

dennis barone

quale press

Some of this work has been published in *Gradiva*, *The Hartford Courant*, *Hot Water Review*, *House Organ*, *Italian Americana*, *The Ocean State Review*, *The Paterson Literary Review*, *Sentence*, and *The Wallace Stevens Journal*, and online in *Not Enough Night*, *Talisman*, and *Theodate*.

Cover image: Barbara Hocker, *Nine Muses Polyhymnia*, inkjet prints, monotypes, branches on panel

Cover & interior design by Marinna Castilleja

ISBN: 978-1-935835-14-1
LCCN: 2015931879

Quale Press | www.quale.com

sound

contents

hammer

Each evening they come back, howling like dogs
And prowling about the city.
There they are, bellowing with their mouths,
And snarling with their lips –
For "Who," they think, "will hear us?"

Psalm 59: 6–7

sound

The knees are the eyes of the legs.
By them I am never transfixed,

but rather transported to where
I want to go. They will never

return me to where I have been:
amorphous or amphibian.

At each turning point they have
never failed to turn: first from

cell to soul and then to something
I have yet to understand. My

knees seem to know what's
next, even in the dark.

memoir

night walk

Our boots were by the door. We were ready to enter the cold as soon as we opened the door and stepped

outside. How surprised we were when we did so and felt the mild night air. We turned left and noted

the right side lights had been turned off, possibly removed, but the left side ones glowed. We turned

left and proceeded straight, uneventfully, though we had hoped to see an animal. When we made our

next left hand turn, we saw lights approaching us. At the last moment, they veered off to our left, their

right. Soon, they disappeared. We heard voices, but couldn't place them nor could we locate their

source. Then we saw an animal, a little farther ahead, enough so that we could not distinguish its chief

characteristics and hence: its species. So silent: we noted as we turned left once more. We stepped

inside and placed our boots neatly by the door, hats and gloves beside.

stammer

Sometimes while reading
all readers fall asleep.
Their eyes close and
for twenty, thirty minutes
the world goes on without
them. When they awake,
confused for a few
moments, they can't
recall where they left off,
where exactly on the even
or the odd numbered pages
they had stopped reading,
nodded off, and let the book
fall, its weight too much
to command. When they awake
they may also, momentarily,
forget their place in the world,
where it was they had
abdicated all responsibility
for matters of state or that
class (soon to start) of twenty-five
fifteen-year-old boys, eager
for something, but not for
reading. The book in
the reader's hand falls
face down and flat upon
a gently rising and falling
stomach. It remains the same,
but has all else in this restless,
frantic world changed?

solitaire

Lines across a surface,
unreadable lines of ink
against the hard white
copier paper. The angle is
all wrong. Even if these
words were those of my
guardian angel, they'd be
indecipherable, unknown.

The stars come out.
But I am in a room and
the stars are not out.
Here is a government inspector.
He has a match. I wait
and while I wait I sit
and while I sit I wish for
hot coffee, a newspaper,
a little something to eat.

In the Strait of Otranto,
migrants without voice,
workers from Africa and Asia
up to their eyes in the
hollow of waves, their last
hope hinged to the depths,
a pack of seeds churned
up by an anchor and not
by a plow, for them:
the miracle of Italy is a curse.
For nothing, they're left to drown.

After Erri De Luca

blackout From a joyless beach
small craft give safe

passage, the cursing made
plain by rule.

In its talking –
what does it say?

Without cards, a keel scrapes
into sedge, stops and

goes with the body
elongated by delay.

In its talking –
what does it say?

The strangeness of it:
such turbid air and one's wish

to know mirrors,
skin and bone.

The river sometimes got so low
it seemed a person could walk across it.

Once a few of the older boys tried,
but got stuck in shoulder–deep mud

mid–river and they were
rescued, pulled out somehow.

Years later I walked out to an island
in it, not all the way across it –

the river, but to this sizeable island,
large enough to tramp around and

explore and hope I had time to
make it back before the water

came in too far and the river
got too deep –

those little kids playing there
about to get swept away.

swimming lessons

at play with mirror

Two kids play
an innocent game.
At the far end of an
avenue one flips
a ray of sunlight
off a bit of broken
glass, the other skips
after that flitting gold.
Always it shuns him,
always it hustles one
step away. Strange,
this play between light
and laughter: their
hearts, content;
our eyes momentarily
charmed.

After Franco Corbisiero

Laura, why won't you go out with me?

We're just friends. Good friends. I told you. . . . And please, stop pestering me.

But, Laura. I think I love you.

You think you love me!

to be continued

forensic   We found him
in a pool of words.

They might have been his
but that is uncertain.

In a city, Trieste or Udine,
on an avenue of lime trees,
when springtime
leaves change color,
I will die
beneath an ardent sun,
straw yellow and high–up,
and my eyelids will close
on the sky and all its splendor.

Beneath the fervent green of a lime tree,
I will fall into the obscure,
into a death that obfuscates
lime trees and sun.
Stout young men
will run into the light
that just slipped away from me,
will take off outside their school,
thick curls waving.

I will still be young,
with a spotless coat
and lush hair that tumbles
into bitter nothingness.
I will still be fervid
and a stripling will slide
near on the avenue's tepid asphalt,
he will balance his hand
on my transparent lap.

After Pier Paolo Pasolini

the day
of my
death

once
upon
a time

Once upon a time. . . What?
 I am so silly tonight!
 I don't remember; but once,
once upon a time something.

You must know it too,
 – poor petal of rose. . .
 Once upon a time something,
something that is no more.

After Arturo Graf

Morning echoes Babel,
a windy planet.
Sometimes others answer heaven.
Every sign falls in a crash,
casting light in our empty window,
white words and white spaces
(white not being the same as empty).
Draw up each day a pineapple,
arches along the line, all
circling in bright letters.
The past becomes a gate when
it flares into spasms of light.

the
new
harmony

a figure
half
seen

Rome was not the firmament
of his imagination. Yet, he read
the plays of Goldoni and remarked
upon the nobility of Colleoni.

As a child he did not acknowledge;
as an adult he saw but dimly
those who would have been
described as swarthy, yet

innocent – unless provoked.
We associate him with a small-
town romanticism, an urban and
commercial maturity, and an

imagined realm forever unseen,
but often visited. Yet, when he
exited an Arp exhibit, disappointed,
a Southern cheese – sharp and

strong, untasted (not Brie),
brought him back to the things of
this world. And when Renato Poggioli
recorded his words in the language

not his, he beamed somewhat
boyishly and then dismissed Tal-
Coat and Oudot, thought instead
of Morandi in Bologna,

an old teacher in Rome. Then
he began to dictate a new poem.
his purview redrawn, and rewritten,
he ascended soon after.

Don't be so naïve, Dennis.
Here, let me give you one example.

My mother lives alone in a small
apartment on the edge of Naples.

My father died when we were young.
She lives several floors up and it is

difficult for my mother to manage
the stairs. She wanted a balcony –

to get some air and sun. She
doesn't have much and this is all

she wanted, a balcony. A contractor
came and quoted a price and

they agreed. Work began. The
workers drilled into the wall of my

mother's small apartment on the edge
of Naples. Then they left and did not

return. The contractor came. He said:
there must be a payment before we continue,

before we conclude. She said, no,
a price has been agreed upon,

a price has been paid, and he
said, they will break my workers' legs

if we proceed. I do not wish
this, he said, neither the violence

nor the payment. There were those holes
and, besides, she still wanted the balcony.

the balcony

That was all she wanted. She paid.
What was she to do: one elderly

woman in a small apartment on the
edge of Naples?

The air I breathe –
a white beetle arrives at the thought

west
philly

of breath in a place I would have rather walked,
if not to the cider mill then to the chapel.

From the backseat I take out the apple–filled
basket you brought back letting one fall as

I close the car door, and our neighbors,
like park pigeons after bread, tussle

for the beautiful apple.

paper
air

The day the U.S. invaded
Iraq you said,
the Philadelphia School had its
birth in Debbie and Dennis's
front room. Overstatement,
but I thank you – and
think that you are wrong.
We did what we could
back in our day:
without pork, privilege, or dollar.
We played softball in Germantown,
rode bikes across Eli's lawn, cooked
dandelions on a borrowed grill.

A ghost story
in which the ghosts
are words.

westerly
terrace

yes and no

In a bar in the city at night –
somewhere – a return
to the rhythms of poetry.

Where love appears
there you are also, beneath
the red flag of gradual, side–stepping

the elemental pulse of a neighbor
for the draft of a thought once
abandoned, but never betrayed.

streets
of
eucalyptus

A caressing hand attends
them: the streets of eucalyptus.
Such pure, antiseptic lanes
stretch across our scorched earth.
A balmy fragrance cuts
through olive groves, clears
bright paths through the darkest times.
One remains in solitude and
becomes trapped in a despair
rooted in stone.
During solitary walks
leaves fall on piles of stones
while high in the blue night
castles glow from the pale
circuit of an unchanging moon.

After Irene Maria Malecore

ars poetica

In my head I hear Marcello
in the midst of *la dolce vita*.

In my head I picture Marcello
in an empty piazza – *piazza
vuota* – a fountain overflowing
with angst and Marcello,
cigarette in hand, staring pensive
but nowhere in particular, watching
some birds in the near distance,
wondering perhaps when a few
friends will return, slowly smoking
that cigarette.

Though I have never
smoked, I understand the semiotic
utility: a man and a woman go
out somewhere, sometime – probably
late, later than I would ever consider
going out (I must stay at home
so that I may write this).

The man
and the woman say nothing, but they
have their cigarettes to occupy them,
to close the canyon between them.
They stare and inhale and exhale
and say nothing.

Now everything
has changed.
They must speak but this
guarantees nothing.
Before there may have been
something to do, but now they are so

desperate for something to do because
they still have nothing to say.

Oh, Marcello, Marcello: here
is an opportunity for the poet.

pasture   Am I now a farmer? Frail, but not
fragile; slow, yet not immobile, I

decide what the scythe cuts.
Mornings are for reading. My

kingdom requires odes and eclogues.
The old songs I used to sing

recalled now by ghost or skeleton are
spirits through which another scythe

must pass. Significant events begin
in exact origins, gray and black,

here a breath, but less than sound —
visible notions of permission — the stone

later. Results show the punch line:
candlelight and music, a picture

divided then carried across the shoulder.

A king and queen harmonize
at the house forever five

miles and myself seem on
lava, wild flowers, a road

grander than sprung evidence
about the grayest cathedral. Cheek to

cheek in cobblestones, dead
earthenware: my friend says

forever to the chariots as fading
masterpieces of our parade

streak the world
with a habitual star luster.

the
procession

folktale

One year he had to do it
on his own. He had learned to
kiss the infant's forehead. Then
he felt a sense of pride. In his
hand he held a tiny couch,
a huge parking lot outside.
He had charm and had spoken
accidentally, it seemed. In the house
overnight the long, hard winter
happened like dynamite. Bees
turned into hornets. One night
was for years, bankable. But the next
day he paid damages, did not offer
refreshment, and set up surveillance
to reassure the three men. That night
he was the only one and indeed he
had the proof. Every year his life
presented the face of a bull to others
all the time to make himself innocent
when guilty. He turned his back and
in golf games three days a week
he had lost and with good reason.
His father fell in love and straightened
her hat, then shouted. He felt in awe.
After ten minutes he said: "that would
be the police." They would give him
a dragon and an abundance of verve.
He shook his head, saw again the
reflections of the mountains behind.
And of course he went to lunch and
played at the table a bewildering part.
He knew certain things: marble floors,
inflated paper, the governor, and
at least six temporary giants.
The right situation shielded by an
encircling hedge would have held
the structure with sentimental terms
no matter how hard the choice.
One was not a serious one and

30

an exercise bike glittered like his
eyes for a moment. All this
he could mistake for the sales tax
and remember on his feet were sandals.
The introductions made, he cut
the house as he heard the testimony
of witnesses. He then explained
the mercy that had been shown to him,
the number and the coming night, the time
to use your brain – the one thing he was sure of.
Let's hear his big secret, the determining
factor! He remained an accident,
would remain forever a sea-green head
cooking dinner, playing a game, crushing
a complete serenity over the ocean,
painting a mountain range in red heat.
His head exploded. He sank to his knees.
He used his key. He looked forward.
He took the time to call. He tested the knob.
He planned the war. He spoke.
He did not mean to be offensive.
He thought of that terrible day. He sighed.
He tried his best. He decided to go.
He made an appointment. He said,
"There is no answer to the question."

war
and
peace

I've rearranged the words on the page

For one possible solution

The harbormaster ordered a bagel and
coffee and took his seat. When finished,
though anxious to return to his duties,
he stopped at our table where we still
lingered and labored on cooling cups of tea.

The harbormaster searched our faces as
if seeking the souls of the shipwrecked
in the lines and creases of our brows.
He searched our faces for some fact of history
unknown to us. He asked us if he knew us
and we guaranteed him that he did not know us,
but that we knew him by his uniform.

He then asked if we were all right.
The question took us aback. We told him
we were fine and had stopped for some
refreshment. Our train had come and gone.
The harbormaster, too, left us. He had
completed his mission. He had delayed us,
and, as it were, derailed us. Now
we had no choice but to travel by sea.

album

Red leaves out from their leather binding.
Red leaves that had been pictures for us.
Once they were in your home, in my home.
Red leaves glued to the album of forgetfulness.
Red leaves from our travels west, to the beach.
Red leaves that we pointed to
and then cried, "look."
Red leaves pulled from the past
and burned in the fire.
Red leaves between us.
Red leaves from the first weekend and the last.
Red everywhere and nowhere:
lost in syllables of regret.

Graver's
Tree Service

Roger Grimshaw
Arborist

169
towns

fragment No temples to Apollo built
in West Hartford, no incense
to Apollo in recent years burnt.

But then up from Beach Land
did arise a path for bicycles:
tribute to azure.

At the coffee bar in Blue Back
one said to the other:
to have done something well once
is no accomplishment, but
to have done it well a thousand
times, now that is something!

And after the twice unhappy
election:
the exception doesn't prove the rule,
the exception proves that the rule is wrong.

Meanwhile, the number of lacrosse
enthusiasts increased precipitously.

Everything runs outside
to see and to taste
and nothing remains within
but a thirst to be vanquished
far from Lethe and Trout Brook.

A bare tree, a black bird, a lady's boot
and low on the roof one word: Inn

in the
air a
sign

shattered glass, twisted metal, crumbled seats
and on the grass one limb: Sandy's

expression of ego or a rare testimony
storms think: knock, knock

our best chance must be the door
let's go to the next town —

a new drama then and some
repetition that is not repetitious

we gallop on strong horses
into the glare of the sun

storm event

It wasn't that I walked on cloud nine,
but rather that I walked around with my
head in the clouds. From that perspective
a gold dome becomes a penny on the game
board. I know how to depict the brightness of
star-shine or moonlight on snow.
Ink runs from my pen as I circle the words
coercion and *inspiration*. What does it mean?
Words fall out of my book and onto
the pavement. Then along comes a train.
What a mess. I have come to realize that
the science of cartography is limited.
Where are words free of shadow?
I like the neighborhood, though. I like
Staccato Street and the tension that seems only
partially alleviated by the mother's final action,
an excuse to run uphill with only a little tepid
water. Her empty eyes empty expression.
My semicolon serves as an oar
used to paddle words down
the page. On the other hand, there are some
definite ways, escape routes, that punctuation
lets me out of the text. Now there is more
available space for the future rather than
a house cluttered with its past.

lamentations

It is the gap I fell into
yet neither a new planet
nor a black hole. I might
have been alone even
if others were present.
And what could I have
said to them or told
myself? I noted the wall–
paper and its coincidence.
We were gathered in our
hometown yet everything
felt so foreign.

Outside the younger kids
rode their bikes north
to the park or south into
town. On Main Street
someone parked their car
in the pharmacy lot to pick
up a prescription and
someone else pulled along
the curbside by Pietro's to
pick up a pizza to bring
home for dinner. Some hike
in the near–distant hills
and others stumble from
the Trackside Inn.
The six o'clock train arrives
and then departs for the next
town. Everything spins
except inside where we wait
still as stone for tall ships
and fireworks, for celebrations
of all sorts planned by
committees handpicked.

I am too much who I am
and not enough anyone else.
What if we confess?

There were years before
we met and plenty of time
apart even after we met
in heavy wind and rain.
It has been six months
already! And if I confess?
Never did my spirits
require to be tranquilized
by quiet and repose.
I could go six miles or
so with my head held in
my hands. I would, too.
I might be the only one
honest enough to confess.
I am who I am.
Just ask.

A child becomes sick and the
doctor is summoned, but the
child dies. And the doctor
arrives on a donkey and the
child's father throws the
donkey off a cliff. The
father moves to America.
His son buys a motorcycle.
The father sees it inside the
house and the father throws
it down the stairs.

Arise, woman and weep in the night.
At the dawn of your vigil open your
heart wide as the oceans. In praise
of God raise up your hands
for the breath of children weak now
with hunger at the end of each street.

Hoard of Jerusalem:
hunger in Hebrew is *raav*,
a snake in an empty mouth.

After Erri De Luca

the library

Absent my cola day here
absent my puppet at the harbor
absent the table absent the edge

absent the image *soirée*
absent the arms career
absent a corona day's riot

absent the marvel the tweet
absent the pain block the journal
absent the season's finances

absent too my shift on aware
absent the tank so late and noisy
absent the black loon I so wanted

absent the stamps' lure eyes on it
absent the aisles may also
absent the million days *hombres*

absent the mouse my new age
absent the sewers the courage
absent a blue epaulet faded

absent the forms skin still wants
absent the coaches gay colors
absent a tan physique

absent the sentences evil says
absent the routes deployed
absent the places key to boredom

absent my mansion reunited
absent fruit copied in dough
absent my minor Etna chamber

absent my sheen go man it tundra
absent sense orioles addressed
absent melancholy melody, night

absent the trembling demand for day
absent the odd jets of mint air
absent the photo few bit

absent a *touché* accordion
absent the front of my animus
absent shock its tent key

absent the victory day surprises
absent the levers a tent gives
absent an Odysseus to silence

absent my refuge the truth
absent my fairest and cruel days
absent the mirth the moon and

absent what solitude knows
absent the marches to the morgue
absent the sanity we renewed

absent the risk that too
absent missed parts absent sylvan air

and for the favor done
you recommence my feet

After Paul Eluard

**even
so**

In the fifth pew sat a man each Sunday who
wore a bowtie, entered unaccompanied well
before the service began, and left without

shaking the most reverend's hand. He was
neither tall nor short and except for that bow-
tie seemed to have no distinguishing

characteristics whatsoever. No one seemed
to know where he lived or why he came so
early only to leave so abruptly. He often

looked up to the rose-glass window and
his lips moved in what could have been
a silent prayer or song. The pew rose up

around him as if a protective fortress.
His feet tapped yet made no sound upon
the tile floor. His hands held but did not

open the hymnal. And the pastor seemed to
address him in particular on occasion, as if
from his pulpit he would reach forward and

touch his congregant's heart. The sanctuary,
a canyon into which we all felt ourselves falling.

Great care must be taken not to
scatter dust, the pasture land
of dreams. Backstage everyone is
cheerful: their shoes like the walking
trees of Louisiana, at least when they
move. Sometimes numbers add up;
sometimes they lessen, but never do
they provide Caesar a pizza. Such
notes of bliss betoken the wastefulness
of a leisure class. Historians can only
speculate from fragmentary evidence
which Biblical verse now must be
quoted. Someone else pulls danger
from his hands, someone else pays tribute.
Return to your book: the rearrangement
of living patterns across an entire
metropolitan area. It isn't difficult to get
caught up with an illusion: the long–
poem all throughout its length
defining terms. I hope I haven't been
calling on your sheet of paper: bold
and resolute. It wasn't my choice that
others sit in one of two chairs. We
agreed, though, that as residents of
Connecticut we would not attend any
soirée. We don't read out loud either.
We sit among a peloton of strangers
where slightly to the left a luminous
quality might hang free from its braid.

mask,
no
mask

lilac

You need to remember
that it was snowing
little words that backfired.
Then you need to remember that
labor is nothing fancy,
nothing at all more than
or less than wing beats
of geese off in the distance.
All the colors of Mondrian's

Boogie-woogie collapse, ever-
darkening our chamber. Now
closer to bloom, I recall
shampoo and leather. The
taste of turkey on my tongue
offers up rough occasion;
some texture to a world
far from those distant geese
and their incessant honking.

Reunion within the triangle:
forty citizens of Paris may exit
the frame; others may enter.
Off to one side a line forms our
boundary of sight. If I could
make myself the *gendarme* of this
scene my arm would rise
as if to mimic the structure's
steel, halt these walkers moving

into and then out of the frame.
Halt – my signal would say
and then I would add "look"
and continue "we are in a
city of lights" and *voilà* the tower
would glow as forty or so
citizens of Paris pause to remember
where they are and I would say
"*ça va*" and I would say

"maintenant" and a split second
later I would know that I had
decided my figure in the center,
the one with the *chapeau*, that was me
turning another image sideways
to see the length of those lines and
across town our mayor counts
potted blooms hoping for tourists
far beyond all accumulated harvest.

Our neighbors have prepared the flowers,
the fruit, and the cloth. I stand as we
proceed down the boulevard and
my little brother looks up to me.
I do not fall as we proceed, as we
march on and on. I find courage
enough to look into our kitchen.
The lights come on as I enter and
once more I hear Ozzie and Harriet

argue about dinner as if it will be
their last meal. Such pilgrims hesitate.
They wonder what will be. They turn
sideways to predict the length of their
lives and their footsteps move beyond
those French doors
and jangle through a sharp−edged book.

sixty   I thought that growing and
         aging were related and since
         I never grew, I wouldn't age.

I am on a park bench
sitting with legs crossed and
hands folded, looking toward
dogs way off beyond the pond.

I wait and think about those dogs
running across that hill while I sit
granite-like on the bench made of
wood, a pebble of sorts, lost.

What we remember may be our
home of first address even at the last.
You call out and I turn but
when I look you aren't there.

animal
rescue

from
the
air

Someone says it is but
you think it is not and
that it must be somewhere
else, somewhere to the north
or to the south; yes,
to the south, not the actual

center. Some say the new
but I don't see it. I still
see it the way it was before
this. And I say a few words
then, often as not about the trees
and how we take care to water

them. Who will listen? I say,
picture a cab moving up the street.
I will look – if today will be my last
day, if today must be my last – I will
see something: a bird on a branch or
a clock – the cars, the planes

and a bridge.

I walk with a chainsaw
under my hat
I hear the motor
all the time

amidst swimming pools
and patios, I see
the tall green tree

ecology

Day to day pours forth speech,
and night to night declares knowledge.
There is no speech, nor are there words;
their voice is not heard;
yet their voice goes out through all the earth
and their words to the end of the world.

Psalm 19: 2–4

hammer

WE SET A DATE to meet beside Bernini's shipwrecked boat in the Piazza di Spagna, Rome. It was a cold morning in early March and when I arrived he was not there. I waited for twenty minutes, one half-hour maybe and then started to look for him, to see if he might be approaching from the direction of the Via del Corso or from the top of the steps down into the heart of the square. I circled once, twice, and once more. This tardiness or complete failure to appear seemed so like him. He would do anything to avoid setting foot in a church, even here in a city full of churches.

I had to leave. I had no choice. What could I do? Our meeting with the archaeologist had been scheduled for eleven that morning. I arrived at San Lorenzo Outside the Walls only a minute or two late. The Professor greeted me warmly, though after visibly glancing at his watch as if to warn me that he was not one to tolerate the tardy. He pointed out the genius of the architects' angles. One felt a depth where in reality there was only flat surface. Then he whisked me off to the farthest sub-level where his students unearthed an altar once used by practitioners of the Mithras cult. Here they would sacrifice the bull, he said. He never once asked where Tomas had gone or why he had not accompanied me. And how would I have answered had the Professor asked?

When we reached again the light of street level, he bid his farewell, apologized that he must immediately return to those lowest pre-Christian caverns, and said to send his greetings and his regret to Tomas. I knew the disappointment he felt for I felt it too and doubly so. Slowly I moped along several

among
the
roman
ruins

streets alongside the ruins. At the point where a patch of blue sky framed by later constructions brightened my view I saw Tomas deep in the shadow of a recess speaking to a man I could not identify. By now it had to be two or three in the afternoon. I wasn't sure of the precise time, nor precisely what to do. I worried that Tomas would see me and think that I was prying into his business, spying on him, and not offering that trust that he required. Two lions marked a passageway to the right. I turned there. I took that unknown passage and told myself to be brave.

IN THE COURSE OF ancient things it might pass out of hand that as long as differentiated thought for every shaken role inclines to think in the framework valuable for a mechanistic fate, to interpret individual activity in the process of unmasking social roots – namely, the collective unconscious – then everything hides which would assert truth is possible through the interconnections one tends to face in a given historical moment. When, on the contrary, all thought rises within a rigid content, the word, we hope, brings us to the men of action. This cannot distort such presuppositions as underlie the transition to that theory we try to mask with categories that are inappropriate, yet everywhere present. If facts can be understood, then an unintelligible margin will have the vital task of a rationalized struggle: elements of our most exposed procedures do not displace the already examined. We should gain through representatives a structure that is unrealizable in closest contact with the present. For instance, to promise that only a complete connection turns events to a structural tension in social settings happens to legitimate the facts to which the findings of the moment would be well to keep in thinnest air. There are two levels traced in this summary of images: the people and aspects of an education. I am not a keeper of things and others have come to bury all those already here. Of course everything takes a minimum of four blocks of approximately six weeks. I asked the journalist not to deny or short circuit me.

the
mind
of
ideas

it's a new world

ME, I DRIVE TO work and get up early to do so, to come down from the Bronx and avoid all the traffic on all those bridges I cross but the thing is no matter what time I get up there is always traffic and the stench of diesel fuel, which is one thing for the life of me I cannot stand. But when I glide through the booths at that last bridge she smiles at me as she has for more than twenty years and I wish we could turn back the clock before terrorists and E-ZPass.

THE OFFICER DIDN'T KNOW if the bridge would hold or not, but after forcing two lanes into one for over an hour he gave up and let the traffic go through in both directions. The date said 1937 and its poured concrete had cracks and splits and nicks in it. He wasn't sure if it would hold, not with the water raging off the old mill pond, over the dam, filling several back yards, and then forcing its way through the narrowing that the bridge traversed on South Main Street. He was not a member of the Army Corps of Engineers and then he recalled that he had read just yesterday that the Corps had its budget slashed. Like so much else these days, he thought: penny wise and pound foolish. We'll pay dearly for all this slashing, he thought, and then he saw a runner approach the bridge, slow down, look at the torrent, and sprint across. Smart, the officer thought. Smarter than the rest of us, he thought as he got in his squad car and drove southward to the station.

And as he drove there he realized that he probably worried too much about the bridge and not enough about the motorists, all of them late for work or school, all of them near the breaking point of patience. It never takes thirty minutes to drive this stretch of South Main, not in his five years on the force or his thirty years of living in the town had he seen anything like it. He should have worried about that mom with the quizzical look on her face concerned that the school bus might never come or that middle school student who approached the bridge, heard the roar, and hesitated to cross it. His thoughts returned to the runner who sprinted across. He wasn't sure why they did so. Maybe, he conjectured, it was because he was now

hero

stuck in traffic here at an intersection where the power had gone out, leaving another officer out in the downpour directing cars through the busy cross streets. He couldn't flash his lights or sound the siren. He was stuck and so there he sat, motionless, thinking about moments just prior to this still present.

He felt the eyes of other drivers upon him. What could he do? In the red Corvette a captain of industry thought that surely a police officer has the means to go and get to where he wants to go even on a day such as today. If the officer of the law had any advantage over the CEO, it is a liberty to feign lawlessness on occasion rather than have to abide to his strict corporate mandate. And behind the cop car a high school student in a Chevy Cavalier agonized about making it to homeroom on time and if he could make a right at the light as it started to change from green to yellow to red with that blue squad car right in front of him. And then along the sidewalk and turning north came that runner again and as he approached, he strode in to the street to avoid the washed out walkway ahead. He nearly ran into the squad car stuck there still. The runner put his hand out, balanced himself a bit by grazing the hood. He looked at the officer and waved. The officer took the gesture as a recrimination, worried that he should be back at that bridge doing something even if he had been called back to the station, even if not part of the Army Corps of Engineers.

THERE'S NOTHING WRONG WITH a man wanting to own some tools. Can't find fault with that can you? There's nothing wrong with owning some tools and a box to put them in. Nope, only way to carry them is in a box and keep it shut. Give a kid a hammer and the whole world becomes a nail. Kids have a way of getting real crazy sometimes. I got a neighbor whose kid sawed his baby sister's leg off below the knee while she was sleeping. I haven't got any kids, but I take no chances. Keep my toolbox lid shut tight as a coffin's. Rather be carrying my tools myself than let some crazy kid get at them, and then me be carried like so much dead weight in a sealed box.

pick
a
man,
any

salute!   WE TRAVELLED TO THE south of Italy to walk the streets of our ancestors. I want to know more than I know. One morning Debbie slept late and I went for a bicycle ride. A ride early in the morning is good for the health. Also, it is a good way to see a new location. When I arrived at the piazza in front of the Chiesa di Sant' Antonio, I stopped and listened to il signor Canio, the mayor of Alberobello. He said, "Everywhere, everywhere these immigrants!" I don't know, I don't know, I thought. But then, il signor Canio, the mayor of Alberobello said, "Italy only for the Italians!" Then I understood. This was a *giro di propaganda* in this beautiful place with these little white dwellings. But, I thought, it is true, the immigrants I saw were like giants from across the sea and perhaps il signor Canio, the mayor of Alberobello, was afraid. He is such a short man. What a world! What strange little cupolas in this place, but pretty and quaint, I thought. I was thinking that I can never know the world of our ancestors and yet I want to know that world. Is it possible? But I am pleased with my bicycle: red and very fast. And just then, an immigrant, as big as a mountain, placed a new cross atop the dome of the Chiesa di Sant' Antonio. The crowd in the piazza turned away from the mayor and applauded this immigrant big as a mountain. Bravo! And then I pedaled down the Via Monte Sant' Angelo and passed many *trulli*. I thought that I could live in a *trullo*. When I returned to the hotel I was just in time for a *caffe Americano*. What should I do now? Debbie was still sleeping late. Very late. I went outside and sat myself down beside my red bicycle, its wheels still turning.

WE WERE WATCHING THE movie and we were in it or else it wasn't a movie. You had left for college and I was alone watching the movie or trying to sleep. In the garage I talked to two friends who I had never seen before or did not recognize. Across the street the house was modern. It had once been stone: now redwood and mirror glass. A tramp entered the garage. He was dusty and shabby and tramp-like. He had red lips and a bad cold and curly hair. He sat in front of us and blocked the screen while outside the rain fell. In the garage someone threw a knife. Let us not become weary, I said. Give us your vineyard, I said, so that it may become a vegetable garden.

penrod
and
sam

this
much
I
know

WE CAN PURIFY, PUMP, clean, install, heat, condition, and paint. We can satisfy. We are certified specialists in filters and neutralizers, hardness, and bad smells. Family owned and operated, we deliver salt and iron, ultra pure; member Better Business Bureau. For all your problems – staining, leaking, bad odor and more – please see our ad under pumps, under excavation, under water, on the next page. Since 1974, for over thirty years, since 1925: family owned and operated for thirty-three years serving all of the valley, the state, and the nation.

We service and repair all brands. Call for delivery, free test, and mineral analysis. We service and repair all brands. We power. We pump. And certify. Guaranteed!

I sit, while out the window morning works itself onto the street. The jugglers juggle while autobiography becomes the pillow on my bed in a slope-ceilinged room. My hair parted slightly to one side. As I said before, cheered up, always. Cheered up, but broken already. Give me then a representational figure, a street where a photographer may flash an image far from the palace gate.

Yesterday my right hand turned the crank of the bubble gum machine and my left hand came away empty.

The next day I walked out. One thing could be growing: not that it'll bruise. For as long as voices turned out, she felt the expectations, but not the clipboard. The heat just was wild, just now. Oh, recollection: who is this *she*? I might mention the same words but in different spaces. You could ask for her and her mouth right then might jackrabbit and you'd just shrug: the vibrations of a mist and a night of tumbleweeds.

And then one day dad came in the living room and told us to turn off the TV and get in the car. "We're going to the mountains," he said. We lived in Florida and so this promise seemed as improbable as all his other ones. But we knew better than to contradict him and we piled into the car where we waited until he had put all sorts of junk in the back: a fishing rod without a reel, a first baseman's glove signed by Elston Howard, two rowboat paddles, an electric fan, that sort of stuff. Mom stood off to the side, silent and vigilant. She waited for him to get into the driver's seat and then she took her place in the front passenger's seat. Dad started the engine and it sputtered a few times. He grabbed the wheel tight and seemed to turn red. Mom started to cry. We sat still and silent. Dad turned the key in the ignition again.

We moved to a house in Old Saybrook on a dead end street five blocks in from the Sound. We had the house repainted. It used to be white and now it is blue. The shutters remain a cranberry color. Dad keeps his car in the one-car garage when not in use and the door of the garage is neither cranberry nor blue; it is white. Recently, Dad has had gutter shields put in place and a new roof installed. He has been on something of a spending spree, because he has been considering moving us somewhere else.

Cousin valued quiet and the stickball games from three in the afternoon until midnight wore him down: the players shouting and the noise of the bat striking the ball; the noise of the boys running the bases or fielding a grounder; the cheering of the parents. He could see nothing over the fence, but from the noise he conjectured a full contingent of two teams and yet that yard had no more space in it than his own. How did they do it, he wondered? How could these games be played in such a small space and for such a long time? He had been driven anxious by the uncertainty of unknowing. This anxiety made it difficult for him to stop smoking.

We can save you. Don't trust your future to a hotline or website. You have rights. We can save you. First find the correct coupons. Print them. Imagine your life! Consolidate; now stop. We can save you. You have rights. Call now. You have rights, automobiles. Don't trust your wig to settlement negotiations. Make the right choice: cranes up to one hundred and fifty tons. The lowest cost *saves you*. You can accept the lowest cost. We can *save you*. Now start accepting. Now start signing. Not satisfied? Speak to a rep. You have rights. We guarantee long-distance packing and crating at the lowest cost, lower than imaginable.

Late at night through the magic of a Toshiba transistor came WOWO from Fort Wayne, Indiana and sometimes Denison won and sometimes Denison lost. Nothing guaranteed.

"We have lost the battle, but not the war." The banner hung across the wall of the old grocery store turned campaign headquarters. Goldwater had lost. We gathered some of the few remaining campaign buttons and stickers and a few last treasured copies of *None Dare Call It Treason*, locked the front door, and left for one campaign worker's house where we ate fresh chilled slices of honeydew melon.

Our town had one Presbyterian Church but it had two sanctuaries (new and old) and two ministers (young and old). The white edifice needed a town green to set it off just right. This it didn't have, but still it was a very pretty church. One minister supported the war in Vietnam and the other opposed it.

One day at wrestling practice a graduate now in the Green Berets came back and joined us for a workout. He had been a standout wrestler, perhaps state champion or runner-up in his weight class. He stretched and scrimmaged with us and then after a warm-down he gathered us around the blue and gold mat and told us of the many atrocities committed by his squad. He spoke with such joy, yet his rhetoric failed him. We were not convinced, but only frightened and afraid.

The schools had been named after former local politicians and I can neither remember the names of the local politicians nor the schools that had been named for them – but for one, the Dater School and that has since been demolished.

Some say we met in the gym and some say we met in the library. Some say you read Cather while I read Pound and that we went to your room and then down the road and the next day to the deserted village on bicycles to see the concrete boat and Jack, its maker.

I had fallen off my bike and scraped my knee. Andy had pulled down a rebound, threw his elbows, and split my lip. Soon after putting seventeen stitches in my lip, Dr. Felice turned to cosmetic surgery and for several years we received frequent postcards advertising the many beauty enhancing procedures he performs. No money down. Satisfaction guaranteed.

peck's barn

First, we brew coffee; we fry eggs; we say good-day and then so soon good-night. The auctioneer will arrive. We've got to clean-up before we clear-out. Picture him at the door, gavel in hand and ready to cry-out, ready to close-down. He'll hit the podium once, twice for the sake of high drama. He'll accept any decent offer tendered. Outside in the old car not too far away we'll sit, not too far away and not too close: what do we care as long as we won't be noticed, as long as no neighbors need feel any guilt whatsoever. Moonlight across the snowy fields and we'll be packed and ready; we'll leave it all behind in the watchful hands of Tri-County Manufacturer's Trust.

"WHAT'S THE NUMBER?"

"Thirteen," I said as he quickly jaunted across the parking lot. I added, "It's a hot day. Good for Easter."

modern aesthetics

"A or C?" he asked spitting to the side.

"A or C what?"

"A Thirteen or C Thirteen, Bud."

"Oh, I see. It is A Thirteen."

"Ah, just as I thought."

He was inside his closet-sized office looking quickly through his files. He looked up at me and shook his head.

"Son," he said.

"Yes, sir," I replied.

"The best I can do is twenty-seven."

"Nothing cheaper?"

"All gone, I'm afraid. With tax, for two of them, it'll come to $64.73."

"Ok," I said.

He spun around, pointed to the tire display by the door, and shouted, "30,000! 30,000 miles every time! Every time guaranteed! Guaranteed! Damn good tire. Damn good!"

"Yes, it does look good," I said. "It's clean."

He directed me towards him with his index finger. He whispered in my left ear, "New valves?"

"Uh, no," I said.

"You're all set then, lad. You're all set."

"That's good," I said. "That's good. What do I do now?"

"Take this slip to the bearded young man standing right underneath the sign that says. . ." and then he paused as if he had to reach deep down inside his gut and wrench the words out of himself.

"What does it say?" I asked.

With the terror of a wounded wild beast he in a wailful voice cried, "AU-TO-MO-TIVE PARTS!"

laws
of
guarantees

I KNOW VERY WELL the implications of imminent debate when placed in brackets and self-described contexts become thinly veiled, a vessel wanting to show which space to fill. What I remove concerns their body, the official site where two ends rekindle (hijack) discourse. I am a total fish's mouth, that toothless fish full of expostulation and charms of transcendence. I know the other side, a nightclub holding the hammer of something many times recorded on the spectacular reality of celebrity. Here the mouth contributes a willful world to recast an existing flame, to extend a base archive of canvas. I have never favored a visible body that edits long the complexity of assumptions or announces whether a tradition fails to gesture one final look around. I find myself being too much the artist when technical description screens language so deeply that even scrap material works into the impossible hesitations of other efficiencies such that others born here since the formation of independent performances title their proximity a part of the fiction that serves as guide. I too would flag by any means my deepest consciousness.

NOTE: THE POET IS consultant for hugs and punches, for standing and climbing, for the tyranny of effects, and the collapse of cottages. Gather all weapons and stand. It is good to be the mayor.

An isolated protestor is he, the poet, this professor. At his home is justice dozing, but apartment blocks rise for speculators and against the comfort of the isolated one. A tower for our city becomes the just cause. Still that struggle continues and the poet spells his words with the juice of limes. He sings hairstyles and lip gloss. It is good to be a doctor.

Towers then and more life and more struggle beginning in 1979 and how to organize the students while today the poet climbs again after five years' rest. Yes, it is good to be a television producer, diversion without repercussion.

The poet for too long asleep and it's been about five-hundred years; so long, in fact, that we get the police to come and strike him once or twice, to try to wake him. Five years then and anyway it's good to be a professor.

A lawyer climbs the stairs. How do things go? Write an eviction notice. Shoot. After five more years, one year at least, then a new house and five hundred officers ask, "Are they still here?" You think about that for one moment and then a politician in silhouette silences the poet. It is right to think for one moment about one's hair and the evening paper and that love of mine. In joining the election there is power for the people and it is good to be a senator.

Was that an animal or a curse? No, it was Thursday afternoon when the producer arrived just in time. He spoke of these things and then of the local politicians. The poet moved to a tenement at the end of last week. Was it any use? And what happened to the journalist? It is good to be a banner.

Have a good voyage north; surrounded by walls, many are content that way. Where does a memorial fit into it? A well for water but the well is blocked. The struggle continues in the periphery without water, furniture, think tanks, or tombs. The struggle continues in the contest and the machine style. It repeats: an educated worker is always a revolutionary worker. These are the words of an extraordinary poet and ordinary man: the general's favorite poet, the one who said, "we cannot speak without words."

A SIMPLE COLUMN OR a set that encircles the field: what would the Princess have installed? We didn't know and hence all our work had stopped for we couldn't move on to the next job without completing this one. These are the sort of things you learn out of and beyond school classes; after graduation.

And yet we so wanted to get to work on the steeple, but how could we do so? We had our commitments and we were committed to executing them one at a time – to completion and satisfaction. And so the church members thought us irresponsible, but that wasn't it at all, not at all. In fact, paradoxically we – perhaps – were too responsible and since we had committed ourselves to the Princess and the column or columns, we just couldn't, as yet, think of or move on to the steeple.

The fact that I take even a pause from our task – uncertain as it may be – to record these thoughts I find – as I write – is rather extraordinary! We have the ability. We have the wherewithal to build a column, to encircle a field with columns, to raise high a steeple once more over the village. We have the zest and the vitality! I guarantee.

Could it be that I fail to see the political nature of my own struggle? The Princess remains indecisive to stall us so that ecclesiological authorities must wait and wait for the symbol of their authority. Recall that it was the grandfather of the Princess, the Duke, who disbanded the church as our state religion.

Woe to he who would try to support the old council – or the new, to be frank. We have an election soon, but since the great conflagration these officials duly elected seem to have less and less effect on any

polling booth

situation, including transport. The whip of power clearly is out of their hands. And while I am uncertain of whose hands it is in (and I am certain such uncertainty is bad for business) I am certain that I would prefer it rest in the hands of the Princess and not the church.

I sense that in the hands of the Princess something in our civil state would alter for the better because in her hands nothing will rest. I guarantee it! In her hands the reins would be engaged and in action and at gallop pace! The pastor has had his hand upon the wheel that guides the ship of state and he has grounded us. He has not destroyed us but he has caused us to stagnate and soon to rot, I conjecture and fear. And the civil leaders – the presidents and governors – attend parades and here I must pause to note how I so admire their colorful ties.

MOST RADICALS I HAVE met were extraordinarily civil. Talbot, for example, the kindest of the kind and then to oppose this paragon of virtue with Clement strikes one almost as unfair; almost as a gesture toward the uncivil and all I said here is to suggest the possible comparison; no more than that and look where it gets me – a morass of dreck. One mention of Clement and poor Talbot may as well be forgotten.

What can be done? First of all you'll have to see what it was if you want to see what it is. Issues of fairness and equity have been raised throughout the deliberations. My task, I have pledged, is to make certain that Talbot be neither forgotten nor short-changed. I will incorporate into my digest no qualifying words such as *some* or *many* but will urge must, must.

When in grade school I knew very well the ambitions of the young Clement. Talbot and I as well as anyone enjoyed the evocation of the flood through the soft sounds of whispering strings: for Clement, though, it was always the cymbals' smash and the bass drums' bang and thump.

But when all becomes clear to my colleagues on the panel will they hem and haw? Will they repeat once more, "Aha! Aha! Our eyes have seen it"? Must I labor in these boots of brown calfskin so that my feet grow tired and turn red with pestilent sores? I am for peace yet if Clement be not contradicted, if Talbot be censured then we must be headed for devastation.

I will approach the choir and ask their aid before the council. These are troubling times. All has been set adrift as if in tempestuous seas. The civil they call rude and the ignominious they praise and lift high as their standard. About the gates lurks a jaguar and wisdom awaits the physic who might remove the ax from its heart.

What can be done? Who will believe our case when the opposition places its placards and mounts its protests everywhere? And on I walk and Talbot must wait, still he must wait while Clement greets the unknowing hoards.

Clement spoke before the panel and told of horrific things: bodiless dogs that howled in pain, ships that sailed into closed rooms too small to contain them and crushing all within them. Yet, he said his plan would return the shipwrecked and quiet the bodiless dogs' despair. Clement guaranteed it.

In the high mountain Talbot sat and thought and waited for an answer to his prayers. He would not speak so extempore. As I left he took my hands in his and he asked, "What are you afraid of?" And I had no answer and yet I was afraid.

A new house will be built and on one side will be an orchard and on the other will be a vineyard. We shall take our books and tables there, our beds and silverware. The new house will sit upon a hillside and be cooled by an ever flowing stream. Though the doors of this dwelling may be on occasion closed, they shall never be locked.

IN TRENTON THE MEN gathered by the Philadelphia-bound train. In Trenton they waited for the last passengers to de-board. Then the men by the Philadelphia train took the last passengers to de-board into their railside tavern.

The berating lasted long into the night. Some had missed a connection and all went without their supper. Trenton makes and the world takes and these men of Trenton would fleece the world if given half a chance to do so. But out of the schoolyard arose a defender of all commuters. She appeared by the tracks and then approached the tavern.

The one they called the Trumpet spoke to her and he called her Agatha, for he knew of her and her reputation for fair-dealing and graceful song. Agatha did not reply when he spoke to her, when he called her by name.

Agatha turned to the captives and asked which of you would travel south and which to the north? For she knew well that from this location there was no transportation east or west: only north or south. One named Greenleaf − after the poet − stepped forward and said, roughly half and half, some would go north and some would go south.

But the Trumpet spoke next and he said: no one is going anywhere.

Then Agatha said, go, all who have been detained. Leave as you have entered. I hold the door open and none shall interfere for I trade my flesh for yours and the Trumpet and his followers will not interfere. They will accept all that I say and these are my words.

And so it happened. The captives of the tavern by the rails left and returned to the station, somewhat shaken but able to travel, to continue and complete their journeying.

And they did so: some to the north and some to the south.

Agatha held out her hand to the Trumpet. The Trumpet – at the touch of her hand – shooed the others away. Go, he said. Leave us. He commanded: leave us now. Return to the distillery by the river and wait for me there.

He placed a quarter in the old jukebox and selected "Perfidia." Then they danced. And then Agatha offered the Trumpet champagne and he drank it heartily.

The Trumpet grew weary and he sought rest upon a torn sofa. Agatha stroked his beard and he closed his eyes. He slept. He slept but would never awake, for he had been poisoned.

Agatha rifled his pockets and took all his cash. Agatha sang: Trenton may make but Agatha takes. Trenton may make but Agatha takes. Trenton may make but Agatha takes – her voice like a swift moving train.

ON THE GROUND FLOOR are to be found a disinfecting plant, special rooms for the vaccination of emigrants, and the office established by the Bank of Naples for the issuance of emigrants' drafts. The plant itself consists of two large steam sterilizers with a capacity for over two hundred pieces of baggage an hour. At the extreme west end of the building are three vaccination rooms, with a common waiting hall but separate exits, thus insuring rapidity and preventing confusion.

Somewhere beyond the sea; somewhere waiting for me, my lover stands on golden sands and watches the ships that go sailing. (Perfect bliss, I think would be to live in Rome without thinking of overcoats.)

Why is it, it was asked of a prominent American journalist, that you print news about Italians which you would not of other nationalities? Well, it is this way, was the answer, if we published them about the Irish or the Germans we should be buried with letters of protest; the Italians do not seem to object. (An Italian will stab or shoot, but seldom poison. His hot-headedness prevents him from committing crimes necessitating subtle and careful planning.)

We'll meet beyond the shore. We'll kiss just as before. Happy we'll be beyond the sea and never again go sailing. (They drive, drive, and drive in lusty holiday furry – to the beach, to Hollywood, to anywhere or nowhere, as a carousel ceaselessly circles.)

Serene was a word. (But to hurt innocent people whom I knew many years ago in order to save myself is, to me, inhuman and indecent and dishonorable.)

So teach us to number our days that we may get a heart of wisdom.

image

run early, run light

TODAY, THIS MORNING, I saw a red-tailed hawk in a tree. I slowed down and said hello, but the bird of prey took no notice of me. And so I continued until I completed my circle and brought all of me back to this ground.

THAT WAS THE SUMMER my mother went to California to help her mom who had been ill with cancer. My dad and I were alone, bachelors for a month or two. My two sisters had homes of their own by then (I'm the youngest) and I'm not sure where my brother lived that summer. Maybe he stayed on Nantucket or maybe he drove out west with two friends in a van. So my friend said she'd cook for us and she made Pizza Burger Pie. She came over with the ingredients and prepared it at our house, in our kitchen. For some reason my dad didn't make it home for dinner that night. I don't know how my friend felt, but I wasn't embarrassed or disappointed. I was glad that it was just the two of us, glad and maybe a bit nervous, too. What were we, I wondered, boyfriend and girlfriend or just friends? This would be a chance to find out. Oddly, though, I can't remember what happened between us, but I do recall – so many years later – that I really liked my dinner. I really liked the Pizza Burger Pie.

That was the summer I dug up medicine bottles from a mound of dirt in the forest and got some money for them at an antiques fair. Forest might not be the right word. Perhaps I should say copse or grove. There was an acre or two to the property: some of it lawn; some of it trees. Behind the trees, there were more trees and then a trail leading to the first of a farmer's fields. I am not certain whose land this mound sat upon. I dug there and got a blue bottle and a brown bottle and others, brands that hadn't seen the light of day in more than one hundred years. For a while they rested on a window sill, filtering sunlight and then one day I

as
you
know

thought to sell them. I got six dollars for one and four dollars for another.

Be sure to short boil the noodles. Use only sauce that you have made with your own hands. Use whole milk and fresh parsley as well as ground salt and pepper in the cheese and keep the mix thick. Make the meatballs tiny, as small as you can – the effort will be much appreciated by all. When everyone wakes up – pancakes.

That was the summer dad wore a red polo shirt and plucked a tan mandolin, picking the edges of his sore. He had been expelled, banished. A shutter of red opened and he plucked harder so that everyone could hear protests more than plucking. He raised his head and I asked for a name or a date but he continued to play on his tan mandolin and I had to look away toward a tree heavy with its own burden.

WE VIEW IT THROUGH action and dialogue. Our gold sin we've learned lies dead. Yet what we did fate willed and planned. He knew it and uttered his final boast: the last survivor not from desire but need. Then darkness loud-tongued forgot the future glory. What must be gives useless weapons. The singer finished then turned fate aside in smiles. He shaped it, bewitched it, laid spells, and blunted fate. He stripped, pleased as the sun had gone. What was right if your hands were hard? No one could unwind in friendship or reception. Scorn and sometimes grace in a world. Champion that the ways his eyes want: it sounded almost dagger-like. Inside an apron and the people were afraid. Start it here.

adam's
apple
everything

the picture goes over there

THE INTERVIEWER ASKED HOW I felt about the task and I said I am daunted by it. I so like what Leah Clovis accomplished in hers that I cannot imagine completing one of my own. And, I added, though I watched repeatedly the Alastair Sim version as a child, I have never been a fan of Dickens. Then there is the additional fact of an early death of a mother (mine) and these matters always seem to be in the hands of our mothers. They are the ones who check the list and purchase what's reasonable or necessary. They are the ones who bake the pies.

But still I had accepted the task as many others had in the past and fourteen others at present or so I had calculated. Mine would round out the number, but I feared I had nothing to say regarding tree trimmings, sleigh rides, and warm punch. No, I felt a certain vacancy of thought and hemmed and hawed as the interviewer probed my plans and intentions. I kept trying to direct the Q and A to those works written in the past rather than to the uncertain future.

The interviewer asked why I liked Leah Clovis's story so much and I said, well (pause) partly because we went once to the deli that the two characters in the story go to. We went once to the same place and had lunch together there, I said.

My interrogator claimed that slim reason to favor any fiction. To favor a sandwich, perhaps yes (pun), but not a story. What could I reply? The sandwich, in fact, had been ordinary. But there had been other reasons to recall the day and the story. Perhaps the story meant something out of the ordinary to me because it evoked a time when everyone still celebrated together and a time when there was something to celebrate.

Was that time a grand oasis at the end of a desert year or a barren mirage followed by more killing, more abandonment, and more destruction? When we watched the broadcast we saw that our planet was the only thing in space that had any color to it, and felt relieved. No, more than that – we felt exhilarated. After the assassinations, the ongoing wars, the protests and subsequent oppression we felt in awe of the universe, of the Creator, of our own abilities.

Too happy to note the foreshadowing of the comment that the beautiful little sphere could be blotted with a thumb, too giddy with prayer or holiday cheer to see that when the camera moved all else was either black or white, we reached out to one another in that moment.

And the next day the guests arrived. My mother wore a long white evening dress and had puffed her hair high in the jubilation of the day. She leaned across the table and lit a dozen candles with one long kitchen match.

My aunt and uncle arrived together for the last time. Soon they would separate and then the following year, in the spring of that year, while I ran around in the senseless circles of a high school track meet someone or something told me that my aunt had died by her own hand. I knew my legs could never carry me fast or far enough and I had to listen when others spoke and on occasion I might be able to reply.

When my mother pointed to the family portrait taken at their wedding anniversary party and said, "Put the picture over there" and directed me with the movement of her eyes to an obscure corner of the living room where no one would ever see it, I said, "Yes, over there" and took it and placed it there and this small redecorating occurred after her return from several months in California and something more than her mother's death must have taken place but I did not know what it might have been though I suspected something between my mother and father had changed.

I did not tell the interviewer any of this, this long parenthesis. No, I said Leah Clovis's story can't be beat. The original Christmas story for the Postmodern age, I said. Then I added, "And why should I try?"

THIS MUCH HERE: this notebook, a baseball tryout for what they told him. Daily observation: they register everything in their notebooks. Too many people have too much faith in the efficacy of new technologies and too many questions about these technologies are left unasked. If it is way off the mark, that only assumes there is a target. And even worse is the fact that every time you cross a boundary you put up a fence. But when the wreath of March has blossomed, then it is crocus, anemone, and violet (baloney). If possible, by imperfection we'd find perfection out (for God and country). Still at the start we pump. We won't call him into different spaces to contradict and grab him. No, we move in a garden on the ledge to this house. Then it looks like he is to sing or else that he hardly slept. We blanket ourselves at the movies. (Critical reflection is also action.) Noble birth: Where did this man get all this? The flowers and demands, the rum and fish hook, and the part played by the word? We'll have occasion yet to decipher the intent.

cupola
and
sink

misplaced I RECENTLY RECEIVED NEWS of an effort to "save" Saint Mary's Church in Salem, Massachusetts. Several years ago the local Catholic diocese sold the structure to a charitable organization, the Salem Mission, a nonprofit that assists the homeless. The mission pledged to maintain the architectural integrity of the sanctuary. Now things have changed. The mission seeks to transform the church into small apartments. Some residents of the neighborhood have opposed the idea. Meanwhile, another organization wants to buy the church and turn it into a community arts center.

The Salem Community Arts Center, supporters argue, would cherish the architectural beauty of the church and would benefit the local area by encouraging a diverse population to visit and enjoy the facility. The arts advocates can purchase the former church from the Salem Mission if a large sum can be raised in a very short time.

Though I learned of this in an appeal forwarded to me by one of the art center's supporters, I thought it a hard one to call: housing for the needy or an art center that rescues a significant Salem structure. I thought this dilemma would make a good essay: it has some necessary drama, conflict. But then I considered that I could not write on the issue without seeing Saint Mary's, and the trip was difficult to fit into my schedule. Plus, I felt inclined to side with the Salem Mission, and hence I was a bit of a traitor to fellow artists. And so I decided that even if this preservation conflict in nearby Salem had significance and raised issues of interest, I could not be the one to discuss it.

Then there was the time I read, or so I thought, about a road-widening project in Avon, Connecticut that would ruin the Farmington River's Roebling Bridge, a tiny artifact from the same factory and engineers that brought forth the grand Brooklyn Bridge.

Here for sure was a good essay just waiting, wanting to be written. I got in my car – notebook and camera in hand – and drove over to Fisher Meadow in Avon. I planned to park and then walk back and forth across the bridge, observing every intricacy and all of its detail in steel.

Such observation proved unnecessary. There is no Roebling Bridge over the Farmington. There never has been. I realized this as soon as I approached the small, nondescript bridge that takes people over the river toward the Fisher Meadow parking lot. I believe that my poetic imagination somehow transposed a Roebling bridge that transverses the Ramapo River in Mahwah, New Jersey, to Avon, Connecticut.

So it's important to see the actual object of study before setting one's opinion about it down on paper; even if we lose a lot of words this way.

dancing bears

NOTHING HAD OPENED YET. Everything had been planned. Inside they both knew already where everything would go and where it would end up and in what condition. For Pat and Izzy there could be but few surprises.

"How many pages do you have left?" Pat asked.

"Too many," Izzy replied, tense if not taciturn.

"Exactly how many is that, Iz?"

"I don't know. I'd have to count them and see." He paused a moment and then said, "It looks like about twelve, certainly less than twenty."

"Can't you be more precise?"

"I'd have to count. Do we have enough time?" Izzy glanced quickly about as if he had heard traffic outside.

"Go ahead," Pat said. "Count them. I'm not going anywhere, not now, not at 2:45 or even at 3:00 for that matter. You see – the merits of precision, yes."

Izzy didn't always get the gist of what Pat told him but nonetheless he would always agree as he did this time. "Ah, yes," he said. "Exactly. I will count them and you can – what. . ."

"Wait," Pat interjected abruptly. "I'll wait. I don't always have to be doing something. Being in and of itself is, for me, sufficient cause for existence."

"You're quite the philosopher, aren't you?" Izzy mocked him.

"Quiet now," Pat would have none of it. "Count," he said.

"Twelve," Izzy concluded, "exactly as I had predicted."

"Bravo! This is exciting. Do you have premonitions often? Perhaps. . ."

"But it all depends, I suppose, on one's definition of a page," Izzy speculated. "What I call one someone else might call one-half page thinking of the two-sided sheet as representative of a single page. It all depends on definition."

"True, true," Pat agreed. "Then there'd be only six pages," he added and they were quiet for some moments. All was quiet, not even the noise of distant traffic.

"Almost a crisis," Izzy suggested.

"If not a crisis certainly a change in the nature of our affairs," Pat continued the thought.

"Should I make the call?" Izzy wondered.

"Need we make it?" Pat replied.

And Izzy said: "And who would we call?"

"The secretary."

"Better to call the undersecretary," Izzy conjectured. "They get more done. Their purpose is less ceremonial."

"True," Pat agreed and then added, "but they are so often overworked."

"And understaffed."

"That's clever, Izzy."

"How so, Pat? What do you mean?"

"You've made a joke, Izzy. Don't you get it? The undersecretary is understaffed. Ha-ha."

"Pat. That isn't very funny."

"No, I suppose not."

"And Pat, what about 'overworked'?" Pat did not speak and Izzy looked around again. The hands in the clock kept turning. "How much time do we have left?" he asked.

"You ask about time?" Pat answered indirectly. "What about space, Izzy? What about both of them?"

"Well, I suppose, yes, they are related, aren't they? Even here or especially here, more so than out there. Here we have a tight boundary around both."

"And they're interconnected, too – that is, related and interconnected," Pat carefully asserted.

"Is time running down?" Izzy asked and once more looked about him, at the task yet-to-be-done.

"And what of space?"

"And the universe."

"As we know it."

"Soon that'll be as we knew it."

"Gosh, I hope not, Iz."

"Me, too. To be honest, Pat, I'm not prepared."

"There's still so much I want to see, Izzy, so much!"

"And so much I want to say, Pat."

"You better say it then and be done with it."

"Why? What's the rush?"

"Time. Space. Universe." Pat paused then and seemed to sniff something unpleasant. "I don't know. I suppose I want to move along to the next item."

"Let's check the list, Pat, and see what the next item is and whether or not we really want it."

"Exactly." He relaxed a bit.

"It says to count the pages next."

"But, Izzy," he seemed frustrated now, "they've been counted."

"Well I suppose we can reconcile then."

"Reconcile?" Pat repeated, confused.

"Our definition with theirs," Izzy replied.

"Who's to say they're in conflict, Iz?"

"'Thou preparest a table before me in the presence of my enemies.'" Izzy recited abstractly looking off into some far distance and then he turned toward Pat and said, "That's in Psalms. In Psalms it says that."

"And that is a matter of interpretation. Enemy or friend, host or guest, however does one decide? Yet, that may be an instance, as you say Izzy, of reconciliation and not of conflict. A table, after all, has been prepared."

"My, we are in the midst of it, a morass at once philosophical and theological."

"How do we get out of it?"

"At the last page, Pat. Always the last."

"Will you be upset? You've been going at it for so long."

"So have you, Pat. So have you."

"Why don't we write something about a basement or an attic and what's in it: utensils, plates, and cups perhaps?"

"Could it be a poem?"

"Yes, of course, Izzy, a poem, a story or a memoir."

"No not a memoir, Pat. Please not one of those and not a drama either."

"Whatever you like then – other than a memoir; that is, or a drama."

"I think I'll begin with a list of the objects therein. Two. . ."

"And then?" Pat interrupted.

"And then, Pat, I will describe the use of each one."

"Each and every one? Izzy, that might take too long. We must be prepared."

"Literature, true literature often makes certain demands."

"On the reader or the writer?"

"Oftentimes both."

"And who do you suppose will be your reader, Izzy?"

"Why, you of course. Pat, you will tell me about all I've left out and I've failed to observe and the objects included, you'll inform me, have thousands upon thousands of other uses than those I've noted but I'll never have the words sufficient to describe them."

"Oh, Izzy. Bring out the squash. They're hungry and tired of waiting for it."

"It would be an honor to do so, Pat. An honor. You wait here and I'll be right back."

They wear their ties as they did on the first day. They haven't always done so. They have prepared for this day as they have for all other days and so their minds wander. Where will they land come May? They recall where they have been and what has been evoked and then they are thankful for kind patience and consideration.

When Izzy returns he greets Pat with a question: "Let's see. Where were we?"

They hope to remember more and more. They said it is annoying. They do not know much about this subject. They go in a car to the station. In the morning and the evening: let it be.

for the record

OCCASIONALLY THERE WOULD BE a word that Cousin couldn't read and she would place an X in place of the word in question. When I received the originals I compared the original and her transcription and discovered far more often than not that I too could not read the word in question. It occurred to me that in the top right drawer of my desk, far in the back of it, I still had Grandfather's glass. I took it out and when I held it over the illegible word, the glass not only magnified the letters and word, but miraculously translated them, too. Thus, with aid of the glass I not only removed all the Xs throughout but did so without recourse to a dual-language dictionary, since the word would be not only rendered legible by the glass but, as I've said, translated as well. I moved the glass along all the lines of the text and observed that Cousin had made one or two significant errors and several lesser ones. These I corrected. It is not a matter of interpretation and should never be presumed so.

They have mouths, but do not speak;
eyes, but do not see.
They have ears, but do not hear;
noses, but do not smell.
They have hands, but do not feel;
feet, but do not walk;
and they do not make a sound in their throat.

Psalm 115: 5–7

quale [kwa-lay]: *Eng.* n 1. A property (such as hardness) considered apart from things that have that property. 2. A property that is experienced as distinct from any source it may have in a physical object. *Ital.* pron.a. 1. Which, what. 2. Who. 3. Some. 4. As, just as.